I0749202

THE UNICORN'S TEAR

TAHIR SHAH

THE UNICORN'S TEAR

A Teaching Story

TAHIR SHAH

MMXXIV

Secretum Mundi Publishing Ltd
124 City Road
London
EC1V 2NX
United Kingdom

www.secretum-mundi.com
info@secretum-mundi.com

First published by Secretum Mundi Publishing Ltd, 2024
A version of this story originally appeared in *Scorpion Soup* by Tahir Shah, 2013

THE UNICORN'S TEAR

A CIP catalogue record for this title is available from the British Library.

ISBN 978-1-915876-08-9

VERSION 08042024

Visit the author's website:
Tahirshah.com

A fine story can convey wisdom into the mind
of the most block-headed fool.

Chinese saying

Teaching Stories

When I was small, I was told stories from morning till night.

I was told stories about genies and witches and about great birds that could carry away elephants on their wings... and stories about distant kingdoms and magical lands ruled by warrior kings.

I was told stories of good and bad... stories of hope and others of despair.

I was even told stories about stories.

And all the while, I listened, amazed.

The more I listened, the more my mind worked... and the more I came to understand that these stories had a power about them, a secret lifeblood all of their own.

They were magical instruments, machineries that could alter states of mind and change the way we think.

But most importantly of all, stories can teach us, without us realizing that they are doing so at all.

Part of the default programming of man, stories are within us all.

Born into us, they make us who we are – they make us human.

Since earliest childhood, I have feasted on stories as a way of learning about the world, and learning about myself. They have been my dictionary and my encyclopaedia, my classroom, my guide, and my very best friend.

To descend down through the layers of stories is to be reborn, into a dominion of fantasy – one touched by real magic.

Pre-eminent within the great treasuries of tales, it is teaching stories like this one that have shown me the path to follow beyond the next horizon, and have made me the man I am.

Tahir Shah

There was once a swordsmith in Shandong who devised a secret method by which to craft a blade that never grew blunt.

The more lives his swords claimed in battle, the sharper and more deadly they became.

Word of his remarkable breakthrough spread and, as it did so, every knight there struggled to get his hands on such a weapon.

As a consequence, there were more wars, battles, and duels than there had ever been as knights, warriors, cavaliers, and ordinary soldiers fought one another to get possession of the blades.

An entire generation of fighting men was slain.

Witnessing the carnage, the master swordsmith took his own life, so horrified was he that he should have been responsible for filling every last cemetery.

But the deaths continued.

Day in, day out, warriors lost their lives for no reason but to fight for the sake of fighting. And with each death, the swords became ever sharper.

Then came the day when every
knight in the land was dead.

All except for two.

The first was named Da Shun,
and the second was called Fu Sheng.

They met on an isolated hilltop overlooking the sea as the rain lashed down. Each clutched a blade that had slain a thousand men.

At the appointed moment, they began
swinging blows at one another.

For a full day and a night, they fought.

But so perfectly matched were they that neither managed to inflict a mortal wound on the other. Collapsing at the same moment on the windswept knoll, they both understood the futility of going on.

Fu Sheng spoke first:
'Neither of us can win at this,' he gasped.

Da Shun cocked his head in agreement.
'So what shall we do?'

Silence prevailed, then Fu Sheng said:
'Let the first person to pass here
decide who is the victor.'
'So be it,' intoned Da Shun.

And so they waited.

For days, then weeks, they waited.

In that time the two knights became friends.

Sharing jokes and secrets, still they waited.

Until, one morning, a wizened old hunchback
heading towards the town passed them.
'I am going to sell my berries,' he said,
'please allow me to pass unhindered.'

Da Shun put down his sword.
'We will not harm you, old traveller,' he said.
'Rather we ask simply that you settle a
score and decide which of us is the
winner of our duel.'

The hunchback didn't know much about duels and duelling, but he knew enough to know that duels took place to decide who the victor would be.

So he said:
'Fight your duel, then, and it will be decided.'

'But we have done just that,' sighed Fu Sheng. 'We have fought and we have fought, and have fought, and have fought, but we are so equally matched that neither can win.'

'I see,' said the hunchback.
'So,' responded Da Shun, 'who is the winner? You decide.'

The hunchback looked at both the knights
and he pitied them.
'There is only one way to decide this,' he said.
'What is it?' asked the knights both at
the same time.

'You must leave this hilltop,' he intoned in a low voice, 'and find a unicorn's tear. The one of you who can bring it to me first will have won the duel.'

The knights gazed down at the wizened old hunchback and they both frowned. As knights, they expected a decision to be more immediate and simple.

'Can you not choose one of us right now?' asked Da Shun. 'The loser will have to fall on his sword.'

'That's the way it's always been,' added Fu Sheng.

The hunchback's face was
masked in displeasure.
'I don't care how it's always been!'
he snapped.

'Very well,' replied the knights in time with each other.

And without another word,
they left the hilltop.

Clambering onto his mare, Fu Sheng rode to the north. And, mounting his steed, Da Shun rode to the south.

Many kingdoms passed beneath the hooves
of each horse. Both of the knights sought
a unicorn for its tear but neither had
any luck at all.

Da Shun was directed to a cave in which a magician was crouched over an iron cauldron. When he asked where a unicorn might be found, the sorcerer pointed into the pot.

'You are cooking unicorn?'
he balked in horror.
The magician nodded.

'Well, where might I find a *live* unicorn?'
'Up there,' the sorcerer said softly,
motioning to the sky.
'Where?'
'In the floating kingdom.'

Hastening outside, Da Shun cocked back his head and looked up into the clouds. Thousands of feet above, he spotted the outline of a city. Blinking, he rubbed his eyes once, and blinked again.

To his amazement,
the floating kingdom was real.

Even though it was day, stars were glinting above the floating city, for it was always night in that realm.

‘How do I get to it?’ asked Da Shun.

The sorcerer rubbed his hands together until they were warm. Then, touching them to the knight's shoulders, he moved his hands in circles.

Da Shun sensed something happening…

… something extraordinary.

Where his shoulders had been, wings were growing. Great, powerful, golden wings.

'Take to the wind and fly!' cried the magician. 'But beware – the wings will melt away as soon as you reach the floating kingdom.'

Clenching his leg muscles, Da Shun thrust himself into the air. He flapped and he flapped, and was soon soaring high against the cobalt sky.

Peering down, he spotted the sorcerer, no more than a pinhead far below. As he flapped, the skyline in the clouds came into sharp focus.

It was capped by the night sky, a panoply of stars gleaming like grains of salt tossed across a dark shroud.

Da Shun rose high above the city walls, arcing to the east. But as he turned, the golden wings seemed to lose their might.

All of a sudden, they broke apart
and Da Shun began to fall.

He fell and fell and fell,
plunging down into the dark.

Fortunately for him, a deep mosaic pool in the palace grounds broke his fall. Before he knew it, Da Shun was being rescued from the water by a dozen maidens. Taking him to the guest quarters, they begged him to be at ease.

'May I be presented to my host?'
Da Shun asked over and over.

The reply was always the same:
'In time perhaps but, alas, our queen has left
on a journey, from which we await her return.'

As Da Shun was reclining in great comfort,
Fu Sheng was hacking his way through
the red jungle of Salanaque.

At a distant caravanserai, a blind merchant
had sold him a fragment of information:
that a unicorn was kept prisoner by a blue
troll – a troll who lived where the red
jungle bordered the eternal sea.

The merchant had declared that the troll,
the most fearful of creatures, could frighten
a man to death by turning its face inside out.

Chopping his way through the jungle, Fu Sheng gained no more than a few inches a day. Each night as he slept, the undergrowth ahead doubled in its thickness, making progress impossible.

His strength sapped by leeches and sores, the knight vowed not to yield until he had presented the crone with a unicorn's tear.

At last, one day, Fu Sheng noticed a breach in the radiant red light ahead. Chopping with his razor-sharp sword, he reached an expanse of empty land.

In the middle of it stood a plain wooden shack. Striding up to its door, Fu Sheng knocked hard with his fist.

The door swung inwards slowly;
a teal-blue troll was standing in its frame.

The creature had short blue horns,
a hairy blue brow, and a face so wart-ridden
and foul that it sent a pang of raw fear
down Fu Sheng's spine.

‘I am on a quest for a unicorn’s tear,’
said the knight.

The blue troll took half a step backwards
and turned his face inside out.

As a reflex to a sight so offensive, Fu Sheng whipped out his blade and separated the troll's head from its shoulders.

Instantly, the plain wooden shack disappeared.

Where it had stood, a palace rose from out of the ground, its crenellated walls and towers fashioned from the whitest marble. All around, the forest melted away and was replaced by a pristine city.

As Fu Sheng stood before the palace,
wide-eyed in amazement, the troll's bluish
blood not yet wiped from his blade,
the great portal was opened from within.

Under the portcullis
rode a pair of royal guards.
'Please come with us!' one of them called out.
'The queen awaits you,' said the other.

Confused and blathering questions, the knight was led into a vast reception hall. Illuminated by coloured crystal chandeliers, the room was carpeted in rose petals and decorated with exquisite paintings of unicorns.

All of a sudden came a delicate sound
of hooves crossing stone.

Fu Sheng turned and found himself gazing at a sight more lovely than any other he had ever imagined.

A lovely princess was riding towards him on a silvery-white unicorn. Her hair was tied back with peonies and she wore a dress of white lace. Smoothing a hand down the creature's mane, she slipped easily off the animal's back.

‘I am Queen Amberin,’ she said in a kindly voice, ‘and I have been returned to my kingdom as a consequence of your actions. It has been floating among the clouds, waiting for this day.’

‘The blue troll…’ stammered Fu Sheng. ‘Yes… he placed a spell on me from which I could only be freed by a blade wielded by the heart and not by the mind.’

‘So odious was he,’ said the knight, ‘that
I slayed him before I could think.’
‘And that is what saved me,’
said Queen Amberin.

She smiled.
'You do not recognize me, do you?'
she whispered.

Fu Sheng thought back
through his many adventures.
'I am searching for a unicorn's tear,'
he replied, 'and on my journey I have
experienced many places and many people.
Forgive me if I do not recognize you.'

The queen smiled abundantly.
'I was the hunchback who sent you and your duelling partner to find the tear and to bring it to me,' she said.

Fu Sheng drew a hand
down over his face and sighed.
'Then I have failed you.'

Again, the queen smiled. Then, gently, she pulled something out from around her neck – a glass phial hanging on a silver chain.

‘This is what kept me safe all these years,’
she said. ‘A unicorn’s tear.’

‘But why did you dispatch us to search for it,
if you had it already?’ the knight enquired,
a tone of frustration in his voice.

‘Sometimes in life the most effective route is not the shortest one,’ Amberin replied. ‘Through calculations and divinations I came to understand a method by which I might be freed from the troll’s spell.

‘It involved two brave knights criss-crossing the world on a quest – the quest for a unicorn’s tear. Only through your quest could I be certain that the conditions would be right in order for the troll to be slain as he was by your blade.’

'But what of my fellow knight, what of Da Shun?' asked Fu Sheng.

Queen Amberin held up a finger.
'I shall reunite you both,' she said, 'so long as you both promise to be as brothers.'

'But which of us was the winner?'
asked Fu Sheng.
'Both of you, and neither of you.'

The queen clapped her hands and a door slid back in the east gallery of the reception hall. Reclining on the other side of it in a palatial salon was Da Shun.

Before he and Fu Sheng were reunited, each one promised to regard the other as a brother and a friend.

When they had done so, their swords were
melted down – the metal used to make a
statue. It commemorated a wise queen
who saved a life and regained her
kingdom at the same time.

For many days and nights, festivities continued in the Kingdom of Salanaque.

The queen honoured the two knights, bestowing the highest title of chivalry upon them. Having been presented with royal robes, decorations pinned to their breasts, Da Shun and Fu Sheng led a grand procession down to the quay.

With trumpets heralding the moment, the knights took their leave of the Queen of Salanaque and her realm, and climbed aboard the royal galleon.

They sailed for a hundred days, across oceans and seas, experiencing all manner of wonders, triumphs, and foes.

The twists and turns of those journeys live on in the minds of warriors and wise men, and in the hearts of children drifting off to sleep.

Finis

About the Author

Descended from a long line of storytellers, writers, and savants, Tahir Shah is one of the most prolific authors of his generation. He has published more than sixty books in numerous genres, including travel, fiction, and fantasy, as well as tales for children.

Raised in the tradition of Eastern 'teaching stories', Shah is passionate about stories and storytelling. He regards the ability to learn from folklore as being in us all, what he calls a 'default setting of humankind'. As well as having written scores of books, Shah has made documentaries for National Geographic TV and The History Channel. He is the founder and CEO of the charity, The Scheherazade Foundation.

Books By Tahir Shah

The Writer's Craft

The Reason to Write

Workbook: Comprehensive, Volume I & II

Workbook: Fantasy, Volume I & II

Workbook: Fiction, Volume I & II

Workbook: Historical Fiction, Volume I & II

Workbook: Teaching Stories, Volume I & II

Workbook: Travel, Volume I & II

Novels

Jinn Hunter: Book One – The Prism

Jinn Hunter: Book Two – The Jinnslayer

Jinn Hunter: Book Three – The Perplexity

Hannibal Fogg and the Supreme Secret of Man

Casablanca Blues

Eye Spy

Godman

Paris Syndrome

Timbuctoo

Midas

Zigzagzone

Nasrudin

Travels With Nasrudin

The Misadventures of the Mystifying Nasrudin

The Peregrinations of the Perplexing Nasrudin

The Voyages and Vicissitudes of Nasrudin

Nasrudin in the Land of Fools

Travel

Trail of Feathers

Travels With Myself

Beyond the Devil's Teeth

In Search of King Solomon's Mines

House of the Tiger King

In Arabian Nights

The Caliph's House

Sorcerer's Apprentice

Journey Through Namibia

Teaching Stories

The Arabian Nights Adventures

Scorpion Soup

Tales Told to a Melon

The Afghan Notebook

Daydreams of an Octopus & Other Stories

The Caravanserai Stories

Ghoul Brothers

Hourglass

Imaginist

Jinn's Treasure

Jinnlore

Mellified Man

Skeleton Island

Wellspring

When the Sun Forgot to Rise

Outrunning the Reaper

The Cap of Invisibility

On Backgammon Time

The Wondrous Seed

The Paradise Tree
Mouse House
The Hoopoe's Flight
The Old Wind
A Treasury of Tales
The Tale of Double Six
The Forgotten Game
King of the Jinns
The Destiny Ring
Changing the World
Cat, Mouse
Frogland
Mittle-Mittle
Capilongo
The Princess of Zilzilam
The Singing Serpents
The Tale of the Rusty Nail
The Unicorn's Tear
The Clockmaker Who Travelled Through Time
The Fish's Dream
The Man Whose Arms Grew Branches
The Most Foolish of Men
The Shop That Sold Truth
Qwerty
Renaissance
The Man With the Tiger's Head
The Kingdom of Blink
The Wisdom of Celestine
Dream Soup
The Skeleton Factory
An Unexpected Gift

The Problem Exchange
The Pharaoh Code
The Monkey Puzzle Club
Liquid Time
Cat Dog, Dog Cat
Princess Pickle's Laugh

Anthologies

The Anthologies: Africa
The Anthologies: Ceremony
The Anthologies: Childhood
The Anthologies: City
The Anthologies: Danger
The Anthologies: East
The Anthologies: Expedition
The Anthologies: Frontier
The Anthologies: Hinterland
The Anthologies: India
The Anthologies: Jinns
The Anthologies: Jungle
The Anthologies: Magic
The Anthologies: Morocco
The Anthologies: Nasrudin
The Anthologies: People
The Anthologies: Quest
The Anthologies: South
The Anthologies: Taboo
The Anthologies: Teaching Stories
The Clockmaker's Box
The Tahir Shah Fiction Reader
The Tahir Shah Travel Reader

Research

Cultural Research

The Middle East Bedside Book

Three Essays

Edited by

Congress With a Crocodile

A Son of a Son, Volume I

A Son of a Son, Volume II

Screenplays

Casablanca Blues: The Screenplay

Timbuctoo: The Screenplay

A REQUEST

If you enjoyed this book, please review it on your favourite online retailer or review website.

Reviews are an author's best friend.

To stay in touch with Tahir Shah, and to hear about his upcoming releases before anyone else, please sign up for his mailing list:

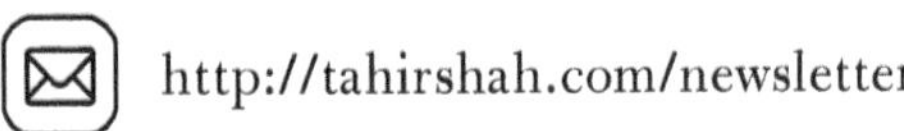
http://tahirshah.com/newsletter

And to follow him on social media, please go to any of the following links:

http://www.twitter.com/humanstew

@tahirshah999

http://www.facebook.com/TahirShahAuthor

http://www.youtube.com/user/tahirshah999

http://www.pinterest.com/tahirshah

https://www.goodreads.com/tahirshahauthor

http://www.tahirshah.com

www.ingramcontent.com/pod-product-compliance
Lightning Source LLC
Chambersburg PA
CBHW030522310726
48979CB00010B/1764/J

* 9 7 8 1 9 1 5 8 7 6 0 8 9 *